# BERGJE

GW01465056

## BREGJE HOFSTEDE

TRANSLATION BY / *VERTALING DOOR*
ALICE TETLEY-PAUL

Bergje
*by Bregje Hofstede*

Translated from the Dutch
*by Alice Tetley-Paul*

First published in English
*by Strangers Press, Norwich, 2020*
*(part of UEA Publishing Project)*

Distributed
*by NBN International*

Printed
*by Swallowtail Print, Norwich*

Editorial team
*Nathan Hamilton, David Colmer,*
*Michele Hutchison, Bas Pauw and Victor Schiferli*

Editorial assistance
*by Senica Maltese and Kaci Tavares*

Cover design and typesetting
*by Office of Craig*

Main body text is set using Arnhem,
Headings are set in Nord

ISBN-13: 978-1911343295

# Bergje

strangers press

# I
# THE TRAIN, JULY

The train took just a bit too long to arrive this morning. Everything had already been said, and we went quiet, waiting for the moment we could be done saying goodbye.

By now the boy will have immersed himself in his work again, and if I feel guilty for not being there for him I console myself with the fact he'll barely have time to miss me; a whirlwind of emails, headlines, error messages, phone calls and problems will render me invisible.

If I ever get there, that is. The rail network is in chaos. The heat of the past few days has caused the tracks to buckle and wrought havoc on the switches and crossings. Even the unshakeable grey trains of the Deutsche Bahn are rerouted, held up for hours, before filling up with lost scouts, crumpled blouses, and surly businessmen stumbling over the limbs of backpackers sprawled across the aisles. I've found a spot between two backrests and curl up to read a book. Beside me, an iced cappuccino has toppled over; every time the train jerks forward, the brown sludge inches a little closer. Just across, an impatient toddler keeps chucking his polar bear teddy around the carriage. A different passenger picks it up and hands it back each time. The mother is embarrassed (*entschuldigen Sie*, she keeps saying, *danke vielmals*), but I think everyone's glad of the distraction, at least.

Less than six weeks ago, the boy and I took this very journey together and I pointed everything out: Look, this is where I got on the train with my sisters. Look, you can see Cologne Cathedral just before the train pulls into the station. Look, this is where we got off. It was Carnival, the whole city was full of frolicking grown-ups drinking from mugs of beer as big as my torso. One group invited us to join them at their long table. We thought all this must be completely normal for Germans. All the boy saw was a grubby platform. Still, I persevered. I wanted him to love Colfosco and I wanted him to love my favourite mountain. He never went there as a child. I know it probably isn't much of a mountain in his eyes. But I wanted him to see what I see.

Imagine you're five, six, maybe ten. A homemade calendar has been up on the living room wall for months, counting down the days. Every night before you go to bed, you or one of your sisters gets to cross off a box. It's a Dutch winter: dark, wet, grey, cold; chapped faces, taut mouths, busy parents, cabin fever. You know that once all the boxes have been crossed off, you'll get on a train that will transport you to a dazzling week; sun on glistening snow, hot chocolate with whipped cream in toasty mountain huts. Then, by the time you return home, there'll be crocuses in the garden.

You leave on Friday, straight after school. The first leg of the journey isn't particularly exciting. You simply walk to the station and take the local train to Arnhem. Grandad's there, waiting. He'll bear the title the Duke of Salice for the duration of this trip, because he's paying for everything and because, to keep out the bright Italian sunlight, he's attached black leather flaps to the arms of his Salice glasses. Thanks to the Duke of Salice, and to your outfits, which clash with those of the other passengers, this part of the journey is the most exotic. You and your sisters wait on the platform in Arnhem in snow boots, hats and ski pants; mittens dangling from your sleeves as a triumphant wave goodbye to the ordinary. Farewell, boring things; hello, mountaintop! Iron-on patches from previous trips announce your destination — *Rifugio Forcelles 2065 m., Lagazuoi 2753 m., Scuola di Sci Colfosco.* My dad still has these on his winter coat, which has since faded from navy to light grey.

You have to change trains a few times, chasing each other up and down the cold platforms, sliding down the handrails, eating an apparently endless supply of currant buns, tangerines and scrubbed carrots from a brown paper bag to stave off fatigue.

At night, you get to sleep in the top bunk in the sleeper train. The carriage is a kind of swaying living room in which stuff can topple over at any time. There's a net between the beds and you do your very best to 'accidentally' roll into the groaning nylon.

If you're lucky, you see the dark silhouettes of hills or mountains when you wake in the night; you're thrilled to find patches of dirty snow alongside the railway lines, which you imagine as the trail of a giant wild animal you're tracking to its lair high in the mountains.

The Duke of Salice is snoring but stops whenever one of you touches his nose. When you need the loo, you sway down the aisle on your own, passing a man who stumbles, first into one wall, then the other, before stroking the crown of your head and saying something in a foreign language. In the small toilet cubicle, he's left behind a smell of beer and urine, and secrets.

The sleeper train doesn't run anymore. Instead, I travel by day and have to change trains five times, in Frankfurt, in Munich, in Kufstein...

Every now and then, I take a breather from the book I'm reading. On the bright yellow cover is a toddler in a space suit. The reflective visor covering his eyes conceals his face. The toddler is crawling over withered grass, reaching for a cuddly toy penguin on the ground. This is our future, the book says. If we go on like this, a scorching hot world awaits us, one in which the sun shines down on us like a grill and where future generations will struggle to exist.

I'm struck anew by the fact the planet's going to pot, and that there's nothing we can do about it. The problems in one or two generations' time are too grim to contemplate. One advantage of being childless is that I don't have to worry how they'll cope, later. I don't have to think: Gosh, by the time this child gets their swimming certificate, the last coral reefs will be largely gone.

When I write it down like that, I feel ashamed. It's a kind of moral capitulation, or cop out.

I put the book away and try instead a small collection of Dolomitian sagas, compiled by Karl Felix Wolff at the start of the twentieth century. One of them is about a princess who lived at the foot of the Sassolungo, a big mountain you can see from Colfosco, my destination. One day, the princess saves a nightingale from the clutches of her cat. The grateful bird grants her the power to turn into a nightingale whenever she wants and to understand all the other birds.

It's the type of story I would have loved as a girl, imagining being able to talk to animals or even communing with the mountains themselves. Particularly the one towering above Colfosco, the village to which my family had been going for five generations. The Sass Songher was my special friend. Hello, friend, I would greet it as I opened the blinds in the morning. When I made snowplough turns at its feet, I'd feel its gaze on my back; a warm glow as if from the sun.

Another thing that appealed about the Dolomite stories was that many of them featured princesses, female warriors and mountain goddesses. Indeed, so many sculptures of prehistoric fertility goddesses have been excavated in the area that some scholars assume this was once a matriarchal society. I loved it. Bregje, Bergje: if you switch just two letters around, my name becomes 'mountain' in Dutch. That confirmed it: I was also a mountain goddess. My name took on giant proportions. It felt immovable, powerful. Not a child's seat, but a throne.

My favourite myth was one about the wild folk. Long ago, so the story goes, the Dolomite valleys were inhabited by *salvans* (forest men) and *ganes* (water women). With the arrival of modern man, these wild folk retreated high into the mountains, where they still live today.

Their name differs depending on the valley. In the Fassa Valley, for example, the men are *bregostans* and the women *bregostènes*. They are woodland dwellers and dryads; they are immortal, strong and wonderful to look at, but can make themselves invisible at will. Bregostans are generally friendly but might sometimes be tempted to kidnap human children to raise as their own.

It felt powerful, being Breg among the Bregostans. Then my name came from *breogo, bregostôl,* meaning 'king' or 'leader', in the ancient roots of the local language. At least according to Johann Baptist Alton, the Colfosco scholar who recorded the myths at the end of the nineteenth century, though I didn't know this as a child.

The people who drove the Bregostans into the mountains were in turn forced out. A different myth is concerned with that. It's called the *Kingdom of Fanes* and tells the story of the mythical ancestors of the Ladins and is considered the national epic of the Dolomite people. These Fanes were prosperous and glorious and ruled by queens. The queens (who had allied themselves with the marmots) were gradually dethroned by unpredictable kings (who had allied themselves with the eagles). The power-hungry eagle kings conquered more and more land, ultimately turning the surrounding peoples against them.

An epic battle was fought on the Pralongia plateau, just above Colfosco. A princess assisted with magic arrows, as did a sorcerer disguised as a decomposing marmot. But despite this, the Fanes lost. The survivors retreated high into the mountains to live underground with the marmots; they still live there today. So the story goes.

There's good reason this story of the ever-retreating mountain people appeals to the Ladins. Around 500 A.D., their language region stretched from Regensburg in the north to present-day Croatia in the south and Switzerland in the west; today only a sliver of it remains. Whereas Slavic, Bavarian and North Italian peoples gained territory over the years, Ladin land dwindled to five mountain valleys.

Nowadays these valleys are prosperous again. Half a century ago, people still ploughed, weeded and herded here. Now they let others do the cycling, walking and skiing instead. During high season, the resident-to-tourist ratio is one to a hundred. So now they are subject to a seasonal wave of displacement, albeit one that generates wealth. The name *Kingdom of Fanes* itself is now also lucrative. If you google it, you can spend hours watching GoPro videos of stout mountain bikers struggling up the mountain accompanied by heavy metal soundtracks designed to convey how they're feeling, since it is now used to promote a cycle route.

For me, the Fanes, the Bregostans, all these mythical names, evoke a certain magic that's more difficult to find as the years pass. As I grew older, I continued making countdown calendars for the Colfosco trip, and I continued to enjoy it, but the sparkle I used to feel from a simple iron-on patch on a faded winter coat, or from the worn-out carriage of a sleeper train, retreated instead to the snow-capped peaks themselves. Fresh snow still enthralled me, as did the view of the Sella massif or the Marmolada glacier with its black peaks sticking out above the pack ice. But I also became increasingly aware of how ugly the run-up to this magic was. How many tunnels, roads, car parks and petrol stations were needed to take us and our things to this summit; how many quarries, pylons, snow cannons and bulldozers made our impeccable holiday possible.

But I'm convinced the magic can still be found. Well hidden, perhaps; retreated to the deepest caverns and highest peaks. That's why I'm determined to climb the mountain I climbed as a child, where I truly believe I'll find whatever it is I'm looking for.

*

*(Half eight that evening.)*

I didn't get any further than Fortezza and the delay meant that the train and bus that were meant to take me to Colfosco via San Lorenzo had long since left.

I spent a few minutes looking despondently at the departure boards in the small wood-slatted station. Fortezza isn't a very inviting village; it's sandwiched between high walls of dark pine forest, and most of the narrow valley is taken up by a river that thunders and foams its way down the mountain at this time of year, full of water released from snow in which it had to wait patiently for months, now finally able to move again.

My sole option was to cross the square and check in at the only hotel, Raifer Post, where we always had a bite to eat before our journey home. On the façade, there's a curled-up post horn from the days that stagecoaches and paper were still associated with speed and efficiency, instead of nostalgic ways of slowing down.

I eat my pizza in the company of a balding badger and a fox that's been on the sunny windowsill for so long it's faded into a more arctic species. Or perhaps the foxes change colour here naturally, brown in the summer and white in the winter, and this one's been frozen in a bygone ice season.

Behind the bar, which doubles as the check-in desk, the master of the house appears. He is grey, dusty and glassy-eyed, like the animals in his windowsill. The fixedness of his hotel is no longer reassuring, it's like a ship that's stayed its course even though it's slowly sinking. Enough time has passed to see how unchangingness slowly changes everything.

I realise I'm here because I need a shock to set myself free.

The boy and I arrive on the last bus of the day, and for the last forty minutes of the journey we're the only passengers on board.

It's mid-May. In Amsterdam, the days are long and hot, but here it's pitch black by ten o'clock and the cold air nips at my nose when I step onto the gritty tarmac.

The bus drives off, roaring and stinking, but we linger a moment for our eyes to get used to the dark.

Ooph. Pfff, the boy says.

You'll never lose him in the dark, because no one can huff and puff the way he can. It's the small words that betray the Amsterdam accent, pfff, so-hoh, like primer that doesn't come out through the cracks.

There's the occasional light in the village; the mountains are no more than a thickening of the black. I turn towards one of the splotches in the dark, the closest one. Sass Songher.

It's 2665 metres high. Nothing remarkable. If you climb one of the really high peaks in the area, this one melts into the surrounding ridges. But in my mind's eye, Sass Songher still stands head and shoulders above the rest. It's the highest mountain in the world, just like my dad's the tallest man in the world.

More or less instinctively, we find our rented apartment on the western edge of the village. The owner has hung our key on the door.

The interior is furnished with brown tiles and pine panelling. There are two gas rings and a small built-in sofa, all a bit too snug.

While I unpack my things and put them in the wardrobe, the boy's already busy rearranging the place. The dresser has to go from the kitchen to the bedroom (pfff) and the dining table in front of the balcony window (ooph). Then he climbs on a chair in the bathroom and tries to disable the whirring fan.

We've spent sixteen harmonious hours in nine different vehicles, but now I feel an unexpected pang of malice.

What if he doesn't like it here? What if he moans about everything? What if it's all a big failure? My thoughts race. Should I have come here alone? Actually, yes, alone's better. I have to restrain myself from shouting: If you don't like it here, just leave!

The true extent of things is often invisible. The one thing I remember about the first time I met the boy is that he wasn't much taller than me, that he had wonderful, big hands and that his glasses were smudged. It was a lot more difficult to pinpoint the intensity that radiated from him in such a way that his gaze became a fierce wind I couldn't help but lean into. I thought of the stories about Odysseus, who caught the winds in a wine bag, so that only the west wind remained to carry him home. That's the impression the boy makes: transporting a storm in the membrane of his skin. Every now and then, a sigh escapes. We've been together for three years. But still, it becomes clear to me now, when I feel how angry I am about nothing at all, that this is more of a test than a hiking holiday. What I really want is for him to find room in his heart for the place where my childhood resides.

I let the bathroom fan hum while I spend far too long brushing my teeth.

The boy knocks on the door.

Yeah?

Look outside, he says. It's snowing!

Flakes swirl around in the glimmer outside our kitchen window. Further on, tall streetlights scatter orange confetti over the road.

*

The next day everything is new and different. There's a thick layer of white on the trees, rooftops, mountains, everywhere, and, because this time last week I was swimming in the River IJ, I find it hard to believe that this whipped cream is really snow. Only when I hear it crunch under my feet do I really believe it. I stomp in it, make snowballs from it, and I'm deliriously happy to hear the boy's gritty laugh and see him stare in wonder at it all.

The mountains are doing their very best to impress. The white has settled on even the smallest ridges on the mountainside, accentuating the texture of the rock. The fact that not a single flake sticks to the steep orangey-pink walls themselves makes them especially forbidding.

Do you think we'll we make it up there?

Snowshoes, I say. Crampons!

First things first, the boy says: Food.

It's still snowing gently as we forge our way to the village. Alimentari Pescosta, the grocer's at the foot of the church, is completely deserted. The fresh section consists of half a mouldy pumpkin and some slimy, green carrots.

It's only after we've walked around for a few minutes, expressing our surprise at the empty shelves, that an older woman appears. She walks with a hunch and her wrinkled neck sticks out between her round shoulders like a tortoise's. Her large breasts haven't succumbed to gravity, but probably only because they're being pushed up unnaturally close to her neck. Only after registering these things do I realise her face is familiar. I struggle to place it at first but she's the same woman who used to sell us the hard, discus-shaped Schüttelbrot and the melting Gorgonzola when we came here on our ski holidays. Because we ate it in such quantities that the whole winter supply would be gone in three days, my dad got into the habit of announcing our arrival by phone, so the stock order could be amended accordingly.

The Hofstedes are here again, I think to myself, before asking for a big piece of Gorgonzola.

Sorry, the woman says, pointing to the empty cheese shelf.

It doesn't take long for us to realise that everything in the village is either closed, empty or being renovated. Our apartment complex appears to be the only tourist establishment that's open, and we're the only guests. The cables hang without lifts attached, the ski rental shop is closed, even though there's a thick layer of snow on the ground.

At Sport Edoardo, a tanned man is preparing the window display for the summer. He raises an eyebrow when customers suddenly appear among the piled-up cardboard boxes. Actually, we're closed, he says, but when I ask for snowshoes, he says *aspetti* and calls a colleague.

I study his face while he's on the phone. How is it that this man has already reassured me? Could he be one of the men who stand at the bottom of the drag lift, intercepting it for you and shoving the seat between your legs? Has he picked me up when I fell off it and ended up sprawled across the track, skis tangled? Or perhaps he's from the rental shop and gives you a push to see which foot you'll have in front on your snowboard, left or right. It confuses me how everything in this village feels so personal and familiar, yet this feeling is entirely one-sided. I always have the urge to greet people over-enthusiastically, to launch myself at them, as if they're family.

I can barely understand what he says. I speak some Italian, but this is something else: Ladin. Ladin is Rhaeto-Romance: a corruption of the Latin that Roman soldiers once used in these valleys, where it mixed with the local language spoken before. Latin may be dead, but there weren't always all these trains and tunnels and Alta Badia's remoteness probably helped Ladin survive. It's still spoken in cafés, on the street, at school.

I only understand the last part of the call, and only because the salesman rounds it off with *ciao tschüss*. He disappears into the basement and, sure enough, returns with two pairs of snowshoes, white for me, black for the boy, ours for six euros a day.

After a bite to eat, we attach our snowshoes and make our way to the valley. The curved V shape of our oversized feet is the only imprint in the fresh whiteness. It's as if we're walking around on big irons that immediately melt a route through the cover of snow.

But it's hard work. Under your foot, the snow forms a compact column that collapses at an angle, taking your whole lower leg with it. You need to keep your leg stable until the snow has stopped giving way and, once you're standing in a knee-high hole, you then have to lift that leg up again to move your foot.

The boy lectures me from behind. You'd be better off shuffling your feet, he says, like cross-country skiing. I try it, but it takes a lot more effort because my feet drag through the snow. He only believes me when I let him go in front.

Ice seeps into the gap between my shoe and my sock, feeling colder as it melts. We walk into a cloud of snow, everything is white; daylight seems to radiate upwards from the ground. With every step I take, loose snow shoots forwards from the tip of my snowshoes, rolling over the surface in front of me. It's the only definition in the endless white. If I don't look at my feet, but straight ahead or upwards, I can believe I'm floating.

Every now and then, I turn to the boy, beaming, and get a smile in return. The cold always makes things so clear, he says, do you get that too?

What do you mean, clear?

Just that. Clear, he says.

I can't look inside him, but I think I get what he means. A body like a glass jar. Space for everything.

Excited about the sudden winter, we want lots of snow as quickly as possible, so we head towards Val Mezdi, the steep gorge that cuts through the Sella massif to the south of our village. The sun only appears at noon, hence its name: midday valley. It's skiable in winter if you're willing to first spend an hour and a half walking over the crest of the Sella massif with your gear on your back, because there's no lift. And you'd better not be afraid of heights, either. Val Mezdi is more of an avalanche path than a valley, a tapered couloir of rubble and ice.

At the foot of the gorge is a sign: *Solo per esperti*. Experts. Is that us? As a child, I used to ski down it but hiking up in snowshoes is a different matter altogether.

We struggle up like two unsteady blind people. Every movement is magnified in the snow. On top of that, there's a lot of loose gravel and rocks on the slope. You never know where your foot's going to end up.

I fall forward and leave handprints in the snow, my fingers forming ten bent tunnels. It looks as though they'd grown there and I'd since uprooted them and taken them away.

After an hour and a half, we've made it about a hundred metres uphill. We crawl onto a large rock to catch our breath, take out a flask of tea.

Opposite us is Sass Songher. Or Sassongher, as it's also called. In Ladin, 'Sass' means top, peak, summit, which explains why you have the Sass Pordoi too, for example, on this side of the valley.

Designations of place are always the most unchangeable parts of a language. Regardless of the oppressor marching across the slopes — the Romans, the Italians, the Austro-Hungarian officers — the mass of rocks did not move and adamantly kept its name. Here, a mountain pass is still called a *Ju* (or *Jeüf*), a rock is a *crëp*. The things the Romans didn't have a name for also kept their names: the rubble avalanche is still *ròa*; the mountain pine *baràntl*.

The rings bolted into the mountainside, left behind from the Iron Age, are another persistent designation of place. They are sometimes mistaken for the iron mooring points of ships from an era when the sea level was much higher; probably by someone who'd overheard that the Dolomites are actually a gigantic, fossilised coral reef.

If these rock faces serve as a keystone for ancient words and places, it's little wonder a child who looked up at them every year for fifteen years also used them as a keystone for fragments of an era that feels long gone.

The summit of Sass Songher is opposite us. To get there would mean climbing more than ten times the height already covered.

The boy heaves a heartfelt sigh.

Are we giving up?

We're *warming* up. Soon, we'll start for real.

Descending on snowshoes proves even more difficult than ascending. You can't dig your heels in; you have to put the whole yeti-foot flat on the ground, but it's so steep here. You can't help but fall over.

Finally, we take the shoes off and run, and fall, and roll down the mountain. The boy tries to sledge down on his waterproof jacket; for a moment he gains momentum, then he falls off and scoops up a jumper full of snow. He gets back to his feet again, shouting and swearing.

While I stand there laughing at him, my left foot sinks so deep I disappear up to my waist. Sound shoots up out of the hole I've made and my walking boot fills with ice-cold water.

I wriggle my way out and look back in shock. Water is flowing at the bottom of the hole. A moment ago, everything was completely still, and now the stream is hissing behind me like a cat whose tail I've stepped on.

*

The boy and I cook lentils with frozen vegetables — all we could lay our hands on — and then stand at the window for a while, enthralled by the swirling snow illuminated by the streetlights.

After a while, an elongated silhouette appears in one of the beams of light.

A fox! The boy says. But the animal has sunk up to its belly in the snow, so it looks like a fish wriggling along a seabed.

Did you know the Dolomites are really fossilised coral reefs? I ask. This all used to be a tropical sea. Thetys. Named after the Greek goddess of the sea and underground rivers.

You're such a nerd, the boy says. But cute all the same.

*

The hallway in our apartment complex is decorated with old black-and-white photographs of the village. Women in long skirts, men in knickerbockers, headgear like beehives. They churn milk, thresh grain, wave ribbons and don't look at the photographer as they sit, stiff and upright, with their looms. There's just a single grainy colour photograph. Judging by the cars, it was taken in the 1960s. In it, Colfosco is no more than a string of beads, houses dotting a winding road.

It had grown a bit by the 1990s. And now, almost thirty years later, you can't escape the nonstop hammering and drilling as more and more villas are built, sometimes five storeys high and complete with indoor swimming pools. Hotels and cafés have sprung up, and those black-and-white photographs are everywhere. Including Bar Sadla, the only café open in low season.

The small, round room is clearly new but decorated with vintage Coca-Cola adverts, wooden skis and snowshoes that look like antique tennis rackets. People are sitting here and there: two groups of women, two lots of men. Their clothing is sturdy but doesn't scream 'suitable for the mountains'; by the looks of it, they're locals.

Before our coffee arrives, I glance over at a skinny woman sitting with her back to the wall. Seeing her face strikes me with such force that it's as if she's spoken to me directly and called me by name. Heidi. That's her, the ski instructor from twenty-five years ago. She is — was — a really young woman, now I suddenly see the wrinkles and the folds of her neck, and that her hair needs a helping hand to stay blonde, the first walking stick for a fading beauty.

What's up? The boy asks, and I try to relax my face and quietly tell him what I've seen.

The shock of how she's aged. Which is, of course, the shock of how *I've* aged; how can a quarter of a century possibly have passed when I see her there now, with those same eyes? It's a rare 'now' moment amidst all those other moments I stow away as 'before' or 'after' — for example, the morning I really need to pee, but can't speak any Italian so I end up tugging the instructor's sleeve, practically in tears, and she understands straight away, thank God, and comes to my rescue, releasing me from my skis so I can go behind the wooden hut at the bottom of the drag lift.

I ask the boy to sit diagonally across from me so I can take a photo with him blurry in the foreground and Heidi small but crystal clear behind him. I post the photo in the family WhatsApp group. I immediately get a response.

*Sister: That's Heidi*
*Sister: From the ski school!*
*Dad: Or one of her daughters – ?*
*Sister: Nejj du*
*Dad: It does look a lot like her. But Heidi will be a fair bit older by now.*
*Sister: Shut up!*

My older sister starts a new thread just for me and types:

*Man I feel ya!*
*Definitely Heidi!*
*Dad's just jealous and likes being a know-it-all about 'his' village, but I don't doubt it for a second!*
*She doesn't even have a daughter!*
*Because she doesn't love anyone as much as us!!*

*

One of the first things I remember the boy saying is: Symbiotic relationships are truly awful.

He said it the same way he says everything: decisively, in a bass voice he never tones down, not even if I'm lying right next to him in bed, as if the volume knob won't go any lower. He even intonates questions as statements. (Can you pass me the butter. Or even: The butter.) And he never, in any language, says please.

Symbiotic relationships are truly awful.

Yes, I said. Because I didn't want a symbiosis, I wanted to be able to do everything on my own. I saw strength and independence as the flanks of a monolith; loneliness was the north face.

And yet the boy and I have assumed habits neither of us used to have. Our specific nighttime routine, for example, of getting comfortable, sleeping, reading, and spending a while lying in each other's warmth before getting up the next morning. The timing of hunger, restlessness and desire is synchronized, and we lead each other to places, like extended dinners and walks where the boy tells me what he's reading and I tell him what I'm writing. I've even started sighing like him. A hundred set phrases and gestures give our convergence language and tone.

Today our bodies interlock on the far-too-small sofa, his feet beside my head, while our minds slip away in different directions via an open book.

Even if we don't communicate, there's a climate of togetherness. A comfortable, two-person greenhouse effect. The boy often seems lost in thought, and I'm convinced he's not paying me any attention, when all of a sudden he says something — a couple of words, right where the gap is. I'm not leaving, he says, or: Nobody's angry with you. All that time, he seems to have seen me so terribly close-up that I only tolerate the vulnerability I feel right then because he's just as vulnerable.

It took a while for us to put those two vulnerabilities together in a way that they protect each other from the world. I sometimes think of two turtles, belly to belly, fusing together along the edge of their shells to form a closed circle.

The lichen is a textbook example of symbiosis. A blue-green, coralline structure on a pine branch, rock or the bark of a tree.

It appears to be a single organism, but it's actually two: algae and a fungus. The algae draws energy from sunlight and uses it to feed the fungus, which no longer has to live in the dark. In turn, the fungus ensures that the algae can absorb water and minerals, so that it can also exist in dry air. Neither would be able to get by in this place on their own.

The boy can do lots of things I can't. He says: Nothing will go wrong. He says: There *is* a path. He says: Come on, and takes me places where I don't know how to hold my own; parties and festivals, because he knows how to. In turn, he follows me up the climbing wall, into the forest and to a house in France, because I speak the language.

Some days we don't resemble lichen at all. Days when the boy and I are completely independent of each other, as if we've each been wrapped up in isolating material. Then I can ask him a question and, after a good minute's silence, get a reply as if hardly a second has passed.

Today is one of those days. It's drizzling, but we ventured out anyway and are now walking down a gravel road towards the forest. The boy is silent. His gaze moves slowly and laboriously, burdened from within. Everything I say has to fight its way through his ear canal, hampered by internal noise.

I squeeze his hand: I'm glad we're having such a good time this week.

Even though I'm *sooo* easy to get through to today, he says.

That's why I'm saying it.

His shining eyes stay fixed on the road. I run my fingers through his hair. Coarse hair, the coat of an outdoor dog. We walk on in silence, and are also quiet at lunch, when I sit at the table and he opts for the sofa. When he notices me looking at him, he raises his eyebrows and briefly opens his eyes wide, but doesn't look at me. I'm always afraid that my visa to his inner world will expire and I'll be left standing in front of this impenetrability like at the glass wall of a customs counter I can no longer get through.

*

The German hiking guide I've brought with me, which mainly deals with practical matters such as bus times, altitudes and where to park, suddenly turns lyrical when it mentions Sass Songher.

> *The massive rock obelisk of Sass Songher looms, steep and unapproachable, over the basin of Corvara, a symbol of bold Dolomitic rock architecture… from its crest you peer down to the eerie depths as if from a magic carpet, perceiving cars, houses, roads and all human trumpery as ridiculous playthings… all in all a marvellous mountain… the Alta Badia's throne of the Gods.*

It was Sass Songher's isolation that appealed to me. Probably because it reminded me of myself. I was alone, even though I was part of a large, warm family.

In the ski school lunch break, or around five o'clock, just before it got dark, I would go out and explore on my own. As soon as we got home, I would switch my ski boots for walking boots and leave right away, happy and a bit embarrassed about my solitary happiness, happy with the resistance of the gravel under my feet and how clearly I could see everything now I was taking my time. I often walked up alongside the stream that is now hidden under the base station of Col Pradat. There were icicles, little birds, tracks in the frozen snow.

Once, though, I made a discovery that made the others prick up their ears. Right beside the stream, in the shrubbery, I saw a chamois. She was lying on her side, motionless but seemingly uninjured, and only when I carefully walked around her did I see the hole in her stomach. The ribs stuck out like teeth around a bloody jaw.

I looked for tracks. Here, look: a pawprint with pads, pads that conceal claws.

Dusk was falling; I had ribs around a soft stomach too. I must have hesitated. But since the mountains had responded to my fantasy of wild animals and forest creatures in this way, I was left with no option but to continue walking, into the forest that started right beside the stream.

I set off along the path that snakes upwards and eventually leads to the top of Sass Songher.

Perhaps it was a wolf. Or even a lynx. Would a lynx be scared, or would it pounce on you? Would you hear it, or would it be so quiet that, even if it was right beside you —

Something darted off, there, between the trees. A fairly large, dark figure, above me between the tree trunks. It was incredibly fast and virtually silent, or perhaps there was a sound, but my surging blood drowned it out. I turned and ran, only glancing back after about ten metres. There was nothing to see.

I always swore it was a lynx. I was convinced of it. Years later, I began to doubt myself. Was what I saw my own wish, only visible as long as I was alone? Or would someone else have seen the same thing?

*

In the days that follow, the boy and I go round and round the foot of the mountain.

One time, we put on our snowshoes and go up the side of the Forcelles, one of the best ski slopes here.

If you turn towards Sass Songher from the village, the Forcelles lies at its foot to the left, a low peak with trees on top, forming a step up to the really high mountains behind it. Its steep rock façade, with stone peaks as pointy as the conifers between them, faces the village, but you can walk up it easily from either side.

We opt for the eastern side, where the lift and piste are, flanked by a wide path that leads through the knotted shrubbery.

I do a double-take as we pass the Forcelles base station; part of the remaining pine forest has been cut down, the tree trunks are piled up haphazardly alongside the dirt track. I can smell the tree sap from twenty metres away, the distinctly living smell of dying wood. An excavator waits, out of work.

The ski lifts in and around the village were replaced with bigger ones in the course of our winters here. We were transported ever faster and further up the sides of the mountain, the pylons rose ever higher, the lifts became wider and were ultimately replaced by enclosed cabins.

We welcomed every new lift with enthusiasm; thanks to the *Frara*, you could get to the Passo Gardena without freezing on the drag lift; thanks to the bridge in the village, you no longer had to walk across the road on your skis; the gondola that replaced the one-man lift on the Col Pradat meant you no longer had to wait for each other at the top.

But the faster and higher we were propelled up the mountain, the further away it actually felt. No more skimming across the treetops, silently swaying in your own seat. No more being dragged up the white slopes, accompanied only by the lisping of your skis against the snow. The howling of the wind was replaced with Muzak in the windproof cabins. And snow cannons popped up on the pistes themselves, their bases wrapped up in bright orange padding so we wouldn't smash ourselves to bits against the machines that made skiing possible in the first place.

The boy and I keep walking.

Where the road bends left towards Forcelles, we follow the zig-zag path leading straight up with our eyes. A low wooden fence runs alongside it for the first few hundred metres before disappearing without a trace under the snow. It seems to dead-end at the vertical wall of Sass Songher, which is shiny black today. Its summit is hidden in a patch of mist.

Let's see how far we get, the boy says.

Just then, something way above us comes loose and plunges downhill, unseen. All around us, to the left, behind and above, the rocks resonate. A cloud of snow forms on the mountain's steep flank before being picked up by the wind and slowly swept away.

The wind has carved shapes into the day-old snow the way it does with sand dunes. The snow has accumulated on our path, forming a hill with a sharp, winding backbone. Up close, the layers are wonderfully scintillating.

We plough on, with more difficulty than yesterday, because each step has to cut through a crust of ice.

A track crosses our path: pawprints too big for a cat; but would a dog have come here alone?

There's your lynx, the boy says.

It strikes me that the tracks aren't pressed into the snow, but on top of it. The pawprints are elevated on marble plinths. The snow that had been compacted under the weight of the passing creature is apparently solid enough to withstand the biting wind, while the snow around it is blown away.

Weight is stubborn. Can you ever actually bounce back from a depression? Or would a gloominess persist, perhaps sticking out ever further above the rest of you, while you live and wear out around it?

If the boy is sometimes distant, I am even more so. It's not intentional, but every now and then I disappear. I get too caught up in my own head. Just as you'd get fed up of porridge if you ate it every day, I can detest the eternal taste of my own thoughts, how my perceptions dictate the structure I place on the world. At times like that, I feel like letting my mind drain away like bathwater, feeling my body get heavier as the water recedes and the drain splutters. Heavy, weary; empty, gone.

The boy offers another way out. I can put my skin on his skin, assume his temperature, look, smell and listen closely to how he lives. Dissociate from my own body and pour myself into him.

I notice new tracks on the snowy path in front of me: two dots, followed by two upright lines. Once again, they are raised on blunt pillars of salt. But instead of a rabbit hopping through the snow, I see a depression on stilts.

Why do I always have to make a metaphor out of everything?

I remember how intensely the world could be felt, tasted, smelled, seen, when I was a child. The fascination with the smallest things. A dead fly: the greenish gloss of the hinged wing case, the miniscule hairs, the suction cup of the nose and the mosaic-like eyes. I was captivated by the translucent wings with their oily sheen and their unequal compartments, which had a particular pattern I knew I'd discover if I just looked hard enough. How many flies have I wiped off the windowsill since then? In irritation, without even looking; symbols of decay, what are you doing here?

The one summer I spent here as a child is as ingrained in my memory as that first fly. I remember the flowers: a square metre of meadow was enough to keep me entertained for a whole afternoon. I collected plants, laid my youngest sister down in the grass and stuck a flower in every gap between her teeth. Every hole in the ground might have been a marmot burrow, everything had a name and a story I didn't know yet. Everything had a potential for greatness.

But gloom is too heavy to carry up a mountain. A ring of clouds forms around the Sella massif ahead, a ridge of snow the wind has piled up across our path commands our attention, and walking brings me back to my own body. Everything my thoughts have blown up to monstrous proportions is reduced to something tangible. Time translates to hunger. Distance is the tendon on the sole of my foot that starts to burn, then throb. Cold is layer upon layer of clothing. Pollution is a chocolate bar wrapper poking out from under the ice, which I put into my pocket. Resentment is gravity on the corners of my mouth.

I wish I didn't tend to forget how quickly my body finds the solution to certain quandaries. I mistrust my body, but thinking is actually more deceptive. It's rarely about what's on the surface. You can be thinking about something really banal, then a riptide comes and drags you away completely.

We are sweaty and flushed when we arrive at the top, where the Forcelles hut is. I know it with a hedge of skis outside the door, with people and music; now the terrace is covered in a knee-high layer of untrodden snow.

Wooden benches have been stacked up against the hut, underneath its eaves. We slide one off and take the bread, cheese and flask of tea out of our backpack.

The Sella massif stretches out before us in all its glory. Today the mountains are black and sharp with veils of snow skewered to their peaks. They really are doing their best, I think, as the boy heaves a gentle, contented sigh. All this glory just for us feels like a responsibility.

As I stand up to lean over the railing, the boy pushes me back to the bench and undoes my belt. An icicle makes a tinkling sound as it breaks off somewhere behind us on the terrace, but I don't turn around, my eyes already occupied with the sight of the boy kneeling in front of me in the snow, pressing his mouth between my legs. I see his feet twitch involuntarily as he focuses his attention on his tongue, hot in the winter air, and then, when he takes a piece of ice in his mouth, cold, so that my eyes open wide and I glance upwards, to the hut on top of the Sella massif where my parents once spent the night before they became parents, and further still, to the peaks above it, until I can't look at anything anymore and just reach for an anchor, something to hold onto the way I usually grab hold of the sheets, while the beauty opposite me ricochets off my eyes, because at that moment I orgasm with my hands in his stiff hair and the boy stands up, kisses me with a milky smudge on his stubble, unzips his trousers and shoves himself between my white thighs, which have little lines on them that glisten in the sun, scars from when my skin couldn't keep up with my growth as I squeezed out of my boy's body to become a young woman, a woman who here, atop the mountain, stands up with her trousers around her ankles and turns her bottom to a man and, if she doesn't say no in time, could easily carry a new, fragile, undefined child's body within her, without the little lines; a body of untrodden snow; a body only half mine but half accessible; something to look at from the outside, something to love dearly but to never again own; on the contrary, if I let ownership be taken of me now, if I don't say stop, then it might own me.

*

We keep a close eye on the weather forecast in the days that follow; impatiently, we see the snow melting away. Our steps now leave wet, dark patches in the slush. From our apartment, we follow the snow line as it recedes. In lower-lying Corvara, on the other side of the valley, the grass is already green. While we wait for the perfect conditions that never materialise, our walks draw circles around the mountain in a continuous, unsuccessful run-up to the top. We do whichever walks are possible: up the Col Pradat, or towards Passo Gardena. We spend the rest of the days at the dining table in front of the balcony window, working.

In the evenings, my blood hums gently in my legs. As if my body is purring, satisfied I'm there, content. In the mornings, it has the wonderful stiffness of deep rest after exertion.

*

The cover of snow is ageing rapidly. We'll go from winter to spring in just one week.

After a few days, the crust has melted to look like tiger bread. The sun has caused the surface of the snow to crackle. Loose branches and pine needles, warmed by the sun, burn holes in their white mattress. A field mouse has melted a doorway in the middle of the path, tracing the exact contours of its tail and miniscule paws.

It's different under the trees. Strips of snow that have fallen off the branches leave patterns like sunlight on the bottom of a swimming pool. All manner of animals add their tracks every day.

When talking of places she's often visited, the boy's mother has a habit of saying: I've left my footprints there. As if you could go and collect them again, those footprints that are yours once and for all. Does walking somewhere somehow make a place yours? I think I've a certain right to be here, more so than the other tourists. But if you see the snow as a title deed, it's clear who signed it first and most often. There are deer tracks, chamois tracks, tracks of Alpine ibexes, even; of rabbits, foxes, a wild forest cat, plus others I don't recognise.

The more we walk, the harder it gets; with each step, we have to stomp our way through an ever-tougher crust of ice to get a secure footing, the surface uneven from the many tracks traversing it.

From time to time, I stop and look for the mountain. Every day, I see it from a slightly different angle and it shows me a different face. But it always has the same characteristic, flattened head atop a slanting collar and flared coat, trimmed with white rubble.

The mountains are either dusky pink, black or off-white, depending on the light. They were once called Monti Pallidi: the pale mountains. Only later did Mr Dolomieu come to study their rocks and give them a new name.

Just like the other Dolomites, Sass Songher is about two hundred and fifty million years old. But every day it starts out young.

In the morning, it blushes. At noon, the full sun makes it smooth, radiant and pale, and in the course of the day the sunlight draws ever deeper grooves in its face as it descends. In the last light, it sits back and proudly turns away; and then, when the sun abruptly disappears, it curls up and dives head-first into the valley.

# III
## THE CLIMB

It's July. The snow has melted, but, though it's warm, the weather's still not on my side. The heat brings fierce daily thunderstorms.

On my first day here, one explodes just as I step outside the supermarket with a bag full of provisions. I take refuge inside a café — now high season is upon us, places have reopened — and stare for a while at the rain, which is coming down with such force that it only takes a couple of minutes before the road is transformed into a mountain stream. The water surface splashes and bubbles.

Then it hails. My tent has an icy frill. All I can do is wait. In the morning, I venture up the mountain and race against the rain suspended above me in grey clouds: whoever gets to the bottom first, wins. In the afternoon, I read and feel the raindrops tapping against the canvas stretched out against the top of my head.

The great thing about a tent is that outside and inside feel closer together. I'm lying in both. In rain and bedroom air.

In fact, all my favourite things relate to that passage from outside to inside, and vice versa. It's usually via words, ideas, metaphors, via a screen. Reading, talking, writing. Sex, too. Eating. Falling asleep and emerging slowly from the snippets of a dynamic, warm, silent dream.

And walking. I can't think of outside and inside being more in harmony than that. All my thoughts while walking have a place in the landscape, because they come from there or get left there. Nothing I think gets the chance to harden; if it wants to stay with me, it has to keep moving. Afterwards, I can trace my train of thoughts based on the path I took.

Yesterday, for example, I walked into the woods towards the Crëp de Sela. There's a part where the forest is much less dense and you can clearly see the individual trees. There are two types: the larch (a type of conifer that's rusty red in autumn, loses its needles in winter, and is as green as lettuce leaves in spring) and the spruce (the Christmas tree). It struck me that they tend to grow in pairs. There's a bigger tree, always a larch, and right opposite it, within the embrace of its branches, a spruce. It's been able to germinate in the lee of the larch. In winter, it has all the light to itself. It's a cosy set-up, and I wondered if I'd rather be the spruce, which is always green, or the larch, which may be big and offer protection, but also experiences seasons, dies off, comes back to life. I'd wanted to ask the boy: Spruce or larch? There are lichens in all shapes and sizes too — long fluffy beards that wave in the wind, rigid green coral, that orangey-red spotted pattern you see on boulders. If we were lichens, what would we look like? And so on. Everything I come across is a gateway between outside and inside, a gateway through which fresh air enters. A way of breathing.

I used to think I had to be alone to experience the most beautiful things. The silence of a mountain top. The lynx in the forest. But these days, I think that showing, naming, and sharing doubles the wonderment. Now I realise I don't have to be alone to experience that amazement, that intensification; feeling safe to open up my inner world is enough. And that's easier in a place like this, which in so many ways becomes, fuels and gives shape to the inner world. They are gateways through which I want to call someone inside.

Now the boy's not here, I'm aware of how often we turn minor setbacks into jokes, how good we are at making things more enjoyable by pointing them out. Hey, did you see that marmot? See those wild strawberries? Or the enjoyment of a book he's read that I ask him about during a hike.

Seeing what he sees always gives me a sense of liberation, of space. It's impossible to get completely 'outside'; I'll always have to view the world from inside my own head, at least as long as my heart is beating. But looking from his perspective, from his head, doubles the space I have.

*

It rains and rains. And then, two days before I'm supposed to leave, the weather changes. Finally, sun tomorrow instead of storms.

That evening, I pack my bag and lay out tomorrow's clothes. The t-shirt has a picture on it my youngest sister drew in honour of our last skiing holiday. The whole family is depicted on skis or snowboard, each member identifiable by their hat and jacket. In the background is the silhouette of Sass Songher.

At half seven the next morning, after stopping at Alimentari Pescosta for a Schüttelbrot and another piece of cheese, I can finally get going. I set off from the meadow above the church. Antares, the apartment where we always used to stay, is behind me. The view is the same as it was back then. This is the only place in the village that definitely won't be built on, because it features on all the postcards: rolling grassland, the white church with its onion-shaped spire, and behind it the photogenic Sella massif.

The meadow above the church is also where I skied for the first time. I was four or five and had practised on the living room carpet at home, my slippers in my dad's huge cross-country skis. That went really well, whizz, whizz, I even got a round of applause, and when I was later put on this meadow in the snow and ended up sliding uncontrollably down the slope, I was furious. It wasn't easy at all. Nothing was ever easy, as I found out at that time and keep finding out, and just as well. Just as well it's not easy. Just as well I'm not a victim of purity or simplicity, just as well there's layer upon layer upon layer; the oldest snow never melts away completely before new snow falls, the mountain unpeels in wafer-thin layers of grit and is always freshly vegetated in summer; just as well there's always something new in the very oldest things.

Today it's the sun, which illuminates the church against the shaded rock face behind it. I take a photo of the chapel and start the ascent.

Just after the base station of the Col Pradat, I see a big sign with a picture of a shiny monster of glass and steel, half-buried in creamy snow. Sorry for the inconvenience, it says, work in progress on the Stella Alpina. While I'm looking, a lorry comes spluttering around the corner and covers me in a cloud of dust and fumes.

The Stella Alpina is the drag lift that goes from the Edelweiss hut up to the flank of Sass Songher. It looks like they're replacing it with a six-seater.

And sure enough, there's now a gaping hole in the spot where I saw the felled tree a month and a half ago. Part of the rock has been removed and workmen are filling the crumbling wound with concrete.

The drag lift itself is still there: a small shack with a red painted cog on top and small yellow pulleys that the cable passes through. Compared with the construction going up with a clatter twenty metres away, this is a child's toy. Straightforward, endearingly mechanical. You can see how it works, you can imagine that it was made by people, designed for people.

The Stella Alpina runs to where the foot of the Sass Songher meets that of the Sass Ciampai, at the beginning of the Puez-Odle nature reserve, a designated World Heritage Site. The new lift goes a bit further than the old one. Right to the edge.

A giant hole has been made in the flank of the mountain on the border of the nature reserve. As I slowly follow the track of the old drag lift upwards, I watch excavators at work. One keeps popping up above the edge of a large plateau of sand and dumping gravel down below. Along the side of this new plateau, a wall has been built from stacked boulders, each as big as a cow, to protect the lift from falling objects.

The steel machines scrape against the rocks; the sound reverberates against the steep walls and comes back deformed, deeper, amplified and with echoes. The mountain grumbles and growls, but it's too anchored to do anything; at most it can spit, but it will be months before it has collected enough snow for an avalanche.

I loved being a child, and this spot was one of the focal points of that magic. Only now do I see the scars my pleasure left behind. Only as an adult do I begin to comprehend the dismal, brutal reality of that childhood magic.

The path starts to zigzag as a steep section passes a chapel for Saint Francis before branching off to the right, crossing a section of rubble and emerging on a ridge above a bare rockface.

From a distance, it's hard to imagine there's a walkable path here. Sass Songher looks insurmountable: that's part of its appeal. The longer you look, the steeper it gets. Yet, when I was eleven, I made it to the top without any difficulty.

The fascination that some children had for horses, I had for that mountain. A big beast that actually allows you to stroke it and mount it. An animal that gives you something to drink. I remember the water gushing out of the rocks, and here it is again, in a depression in the wall. The smell, sound and colour changed in an instant: rusty yellow mosses, a gentle gushing and gurgling, the rocks dark from the moisture.

The rest of the mountain is bare and stony, dotted with coarse grass and flowers. There are pale yellow ones with dark yellow hearts, and elongated purple trumpets. The higher you go, the sparser the vegetation, until all that's left is a robust moss with miniature purple flowers. After that, there's only the white gravel of the *monte pallido* itself.

Every now and then, I'm startled when the mountain growls at me, but the rubble I expect to come tumbling down never does; I'm just hearing the echoes of the demolition and construction work in the valley. It follows me as I traverse the shoulder. Only when I reach the pass and climb along the neck to the crown of its head do I leave the sounds of the machinery behind.

Before the final, steep climb, the mountain offers me a view of its spiky dorsal fin; the *torri del Sass Songher* and a sharp, narrow gorge separate the mountain from its hinterland. From the pass, you can just see into the next valley, but the village underneath it remains hidden.

Someone has installed a cable in the rock here, a *via ferrata* to bridge the steepest part of the climb. The twisted steel cuts into the palms of my hands.

Another few hundred metres. I look forward to finally reaching the top; you've spent hours staring at the rocks ahead and at the slope that's persistently blocked your view. For as long as you keep plodding on up it, your flank is the only one. And then, within a few steps, the landscape behind it appears and the world doubles in size.

It's already busy when I reach the top. Three couples loiter near the cross on the summit, walk carefully on the small peak, take pictures. They greet me. There's a young man on a video call. He walks around, stepping over the steel wire that holds the cross in place while he chats enthusiastically to a woman who looks like his mother. I keep a nervous eye on his feet, worried that this woman will see her son go plummeting off the edge in real time.

The cross I remember, a rough steel, stone-filled construction, has been replaced. Only the base is still visible, embedded into the rock. A new cross, a more modern and uglier one, has been erected right beside it. It's held upright by taut steel wire, which hums and sings whenever someone touches it. It can't be all that new, because the photo that someone's stuck to the inside of it has already faded. You can still just about make out the two men standing arm in arm, one young, the other old.

At the edge of the summit, a boulder the size of a small car has come loose. You can tell from its ochre colour that the break is still fresh. Although the fragment is still balancing, it could go crashing down towards Col Pradat at any moment.

I eat my bread and cheese huddled inside my down jacket to protect me from the sudden wind. In the distance, to the north, are the snow-covered Alps, bleak, regular in shape. Closer, to their left, is the swirling stone plateau of the Gherdenacia, which looks more like molten lava than a former seabed. If you turn and look down over Colfosco, you'll see the jagged peaks of the Dolomites. There's the Marmolada Glacier, which looks like the spiky lower jaw of a dinosaur, its stone teeth embedded in icy, receding gums.

I hate to admit it, but I'm disappointed. I'd rather have done the hikes of the past days. They were silent, shady. A view through the trees, little creatures on the path.

While I rub my hands over my cold legs, I think back to a moment two days ago. I'd hiked up to the Crëp de Münt and was having my lunch at the top of an idle ski lift. When I unfolded the map on my knees, my bare feet in the grass and a piece of bread in my mouth, a bright green beetle with a sea-green shell that looked like it had been dipped in glitter landed on it. In a matter of seconds, it walked from Selva over the flank of Sass Songher to the edge of the map. It stopped, raised its shells and flew off, swerving when the wind got a hold on it.

Something so small. And yet it was bigger than today's journey. Here was miniature perfection, sparkling sea-green, extraordinary and gone in a flash.

I've been kidding myself, I think, spending weeks fixated on a route, when a beetle can hop straight across it with giant steps. What I'm looking for doesn't appear to be where it was, not at the top but instead in the detour, amongst the frustrations.

I always thought I had to live an exciting and remarkable life, that I had to seek out a summit so as to touch the intensity that electrifies me and keeps me going for weeks. I thought the daily grind (the repetition, the ordinary, the unremarkable) caused layers of dust. Now I think: No, it's haste that keeps me from seeing the sparkle. The haste to get to the top.

I don't have to revisit old, sacred sites of my past. I can start something new and go where I want. In fact, I'll have to. Lightning never strikes the same place twice. The spark moves, and that's what sets me free.

All of a sudden, I get a sharp pain in my tummy. For a moment, I think it's the food. Then I recognise the cramp and count back the days.

And I'm wearing a skirt to top it off.

But hang on a moment. Look around, Bregje. Isn't this what you came for? I gaze at the highest rocky outcrops, softly say their names. Lagazuoi, Sasso Lungo, Sas Ciampac, Sas Ciampai, Col de Puez, Col Turot, Cima Pisciadù, Col Aut. But I've got to go down.

The summit is forbidding. Small, bare, windy, gritty, without any shelter. And busy. Another two people have arrived, and I meet a group of a good twenty hikers in the first two hundred metres of my descent. It's at least fifteen minutes before I can hide between two boulders and put a tampon in before continuing, a red cotton tail between my legs.

*

The night before my departure, I wake at around four to pee.
I grope for my glasses in the side pocket, unzip the inner tent,
and freeze.

It doesn't make sense.

I sit there for a moment, half asleep, not entirely sure if this is the
aftermath of a dream. Then it hits me: the porch is emptier than it
should be. All the food is gone.

I unzip the outer tent. In the powdery dawn light I see all my
possessions reduced to rubbish. Here's a piece of plastic. There's a
supermarket receipt. Further along, the white wax paper in which I'd
wrapped a big chunk of Gorgonzola the night before; further still, the
Parmesan cheese packet.

I crawl out of my tent and start collecting it all, a shredded eggbox
the only evidence of the eggs I'd hardboiled yesterday for the train.
The yoghurt pot has been slurped dry. And at the end of the trail,
beside the canvas bag that once contained all of this, I see the pointy
outline of an animal. A sloping back, a long, full tail. It looks at me,
I see the green sheen of the membrane behind its eyes. Then it darts
off, back into the forest.

**nieuw** new
dutch **nederlands**
**stemmen** voices

VERZET is a series of chapbooks showcasing the work of some of the most exciting writers working in Dutch today, published by Strangers Press, part of the UEA Publishing Project.

Each story is beautifully translated and presented as an individual chapbook, with a design inspired by the text in collaboration with The Dutch Foundation for Literature and National Centre for Writing.

Supported by

**N** National Centre
for Writing

**N** ederlands
letterenfonds
dutch foundation
for literature

This series was made possible by generous funding from The Dutch Foundation for Literature